THE SPARROW'S SONG

Ian Wallace

A Meadow Mouse Paperback
Groundwood/Douglas & McIntyre Ltd.
585 Bloor Street West
Toronto, Ontario M6G 1K5

Canadian Cataloguing in Publication Data

Wallace, Ian, 1950–
    The sparrow's song

"A Meadowmouse paperback".
ISBN 0-88899-204-1

I. Title.

PS8595.A566S62 1994   jC813'.54 C94-930509-X
PZ7.W35Sp 1994

Printed and bound in Hong Kong
by Everbest Printing Co., Ltd.

A Meadow Mouse Paperback

Groundwood/Douglas & McIntyre

Toronto/Vancouver/Buffalo

To my mother, who kept this story alive

Katie was fishing one early summer's day when the stillness was broken by a hollow thwack. A song sparrow fell from the sky and into the creek with a splash that told her it was dead.

She made a boat of willow reeds, laid the bird inside and set the boat adrift. Then, from somewhere along the bank, a young sparrow fluttered helplessly down toward her, calling for its mother.

Katie scooped the baby bird into her fisherman's hat and turned to go. There stood her brother Charles, clutching his slingshot and a bag of stones.

"It's only a sparrow," he said.

"And you're just a little boy," Katie snapped, and she raced away from the creek toward home.

Safe indoors, Katie tucked the sparrow inside a cage that she found in the attic. The frightened bird curled up into a tight, trembling ball. Slowly, tenderly, Katie coaxed it out. Her warm voice began to ease the sparrow's fears and it gobbled up a morsel of bread from her fingers, hungrily crying out, "More."

As the days passed, the bird's breast feathers darkened beneath wings that grew straight and strong. Not once did Katie let Charles near. When she saw the bird attempting to fly, she carried its cage to the edge of the city nearby and down the winding road that led into the mythic gorge beyond . . .

"This is the most magical place I know," she said, and let the sparrow hop along the ground to feel the touch of rocks and grass.

She wove a nest of twigs and leaves and dandelions and set the bird inside. The thundering mist roaring and rising behind her, Katie began to sing. Her song, soft and low, took flight the moment the sparrow joined in, and their voices rippled like sunlight off the walls of the gorge.

Without warning, Charles appeared on the riverbank. Forgetting the cage, Katie was off in a flash. But her brother was quick. In no time at all he was upon her.

"How long do I have to be sorry?" he demanded.

"Until you're a hundred and four!"

Charles caught her hard and spun her around.

"I never meant to kill its mother," he said sadly.

Katie and Charles stood locked in a silent grip. Suddenly, the sparrow left its nest, struggling to fly away, but its wings carried it only as far as the top of Charles's head.

Katie laughed so hard that she forgave her brother at last.

"Now," she said, perching the bird on her finger, "we'll teach you to fly, long and high . . ."

As June turned into July, Katie and Charles searched the creek every morning for worms, insects and larvae. While they worked, the sparrow trilled contentedly beside them.

Soon the bird's wings carried it high above the trees, and their mother entered their world with a challenge they could not ignore.

"It's time to let it go," she told them.

"I don't want to," they answered in one voice.

"Just set it free in a safe place. Then you'll always think of it there."

Not long after, Katie and Charles returned to the gorge.
Katie held the cage to her breast one last time. She
unlatched the door, and the sparrow swooped into

the welcoming sky. Beating its wings against the fateful
wind, the bird soared triumphantly, long and high.

From his pocket Charles pulled his slingshot. Katie gasped in fear, but instead of aiming the slingshot, Charles hurled it away. End over end it tumbled through the air until the river swallowed it up.

Before the sparrow could return, they stole hastily away.

In the days of late summer, Katie and Charles fished the creek, their thoughts of the sparrow drifting on the current. Did it have enough to eat? Had it found a mate and a sheltered place to nest? Once Charles dared to ask, "Do you think it will live without us?"

Katie shook off his question as she tugged on her line. "No fish today," she said while, inside, she prayed.

The day fall arrived on the creek, Katie and Charles were playing checkers. They studied each move with such care that they barely heard a bird singing outside the open window.

A long time passed before they looked up from their game. Then, in a flash, they recognized the song of their sparrow.

"That's our bird!" Katie called out, and they followed the song to the maple tree in their yard. The tiny bird flew down from its perch and landed on Katie's outstretched finger.

"Do you know what a sparrow says when it sings?" asked Katie.

"No, what?"

" 'I'm fine . . . I'm fine.' Our sparrow came back to tell us that."

As darkness fell, the sparrow flew away. Katie and Charles never saw it again. But whenever they heard a sparrow trill, they could imagine their bird zig-zagging high above Niagara Falls.